WE BOTH READ®

Parent's Introduction

We Both Read is the first series of books designed to invite parents and children to share the reading of a story by taking turns reading aloud. This "shared reading" innovation, which was developed in conjunction with early reading specialists, invites parents to read the more sophisticated text on the left-hand pages, while children are encouraged to read the right-hand pages, which have been written at one of three early reading levels.

Reading aloud is one of the most important activities parents can share with their child to assist their reading development. However, *We Both Read* goes beyond reading *to* a child and allows parents to share reading *with* a child. *We Both Read* is so powerful and effective because it combines two key elements in learning: "showing" (the parent reads) and "doing" (the child reads). The result is not only faster reading development for the child, but a much more enjoyable and enriching experience for both!

Most of the words used in the child's text should be familiar to them. Others can easily be sounded out. An occasional difficult word will be first introduced in the parent's text, distinguished with **bold lettering**. Pointing out these words, as you read them, will help familiarize them to your child. You may also find it helpful to read the entire book aloud yourself the first time, then invite your child to participate on the second reading. Also note that the parent's text is preceded by a "talking parent" icon: ⊖ ; and the child's text is preceded by a "talking child" icon: ⊙ .

We Both Read books is a fun, easy way to encourage and help your child to read — and a wonderful way to start your child off on a lifetime of reading enjoyment!

We Both Read: Baseball Fever

_____

We Both Read® is a registered trademark of Treasure Bay, Inc.

Published by Treasure Bay, Inc.
17 Parkgrove Drive
South San Francisco, CA 94080 USA

PRINTED IN SINGAPORE

Library of Congress Catalog Card Number: 2002094713

Hardcover ISBN: 1-891327-45-3
Paperback ISBN: 1-891327-46-1

FIRST EDITION

We Both Read® Books
Patent No. 5,957,693

WE BOTH READ®

Baseball Fever

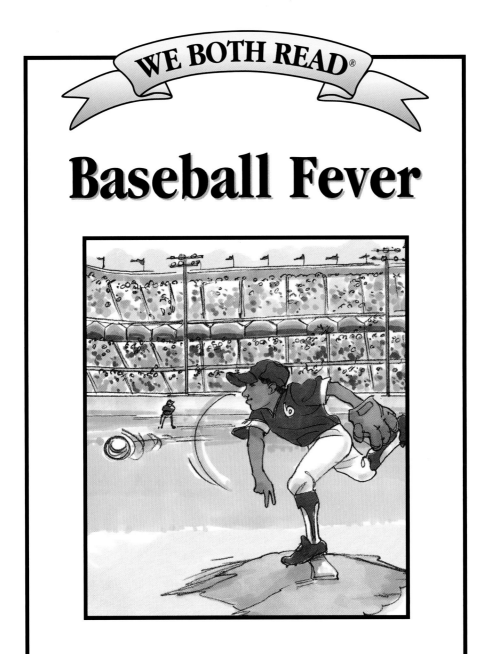

By Sindy McKay

Illustrated by Meredith Johnson

TREASURE BAY

The clock in my classroom moved slowly toward three o'clock. It **always** moved slowly on baseball practice days.

BBRRRIIIING! The dismissal bell finally rang! I grabbed up my backpack and raced out toward the field as fast as I could go!

I was going to be the first one there. I was **always** the first one there.

But I wasn't the first one there today.

Karen Washington, the best shortstop in the league, was there before me. She waved and yelled, "Hi Jason!"

I answered her with a great big sneeze!

"Whoa, are you okay?" she asked.

I told her I was fine. Then I ran to the **pitcher's** mound to get in some practice before Coach Bill arrived.

Coach Bill was a great coach. He made our team a great team. He made me a great **pitcher!**

Coach Bill sent four of us to the outfield while the rest of the team lined up for batting practice. Karen stepped up and hit a high fly, right to me.

"I've got it!" I called as I positioned myself beneath the ball. And then I **sneezed.**

I **sneezed** hard. Then I sneezed again. And I sneezed once more.

The ball hit the dirt at my feet.

Coach Bill ran out to see if I was okay.

"Looks like you're getting sick, Jason," he announced. "You better go home and take care of yourself. Saturday is our first game of the season and I don't want you to miss it!"

I didn't want to go home. But Coach Bill said I had to.

I didn't want to be sick. But I was.

That night at dinner, Mom noticed I wasn't eating my peas. I usually love peas—but they tasted kind of yucky tonight. Mom frowned and reached across the table to feel my forehead. "Do you feel okay, son?"

"I feel fine," I said. "I feel great!" And then
I sneezed again.

Mom sent me right to bed.

When I woke up the next morning I didn't feel too **terrific.**
My throat was scratchy and my nose was stuffy and I didn't
feel like going to school or to **baseball practice** or anything. I
just wanted to crawl under my covers and go back to sleep.

Mom came in my room. I told her I felt **terrific!** "I can't wait to go to school," I said. "I can't wait to go to **baseball practice.**"

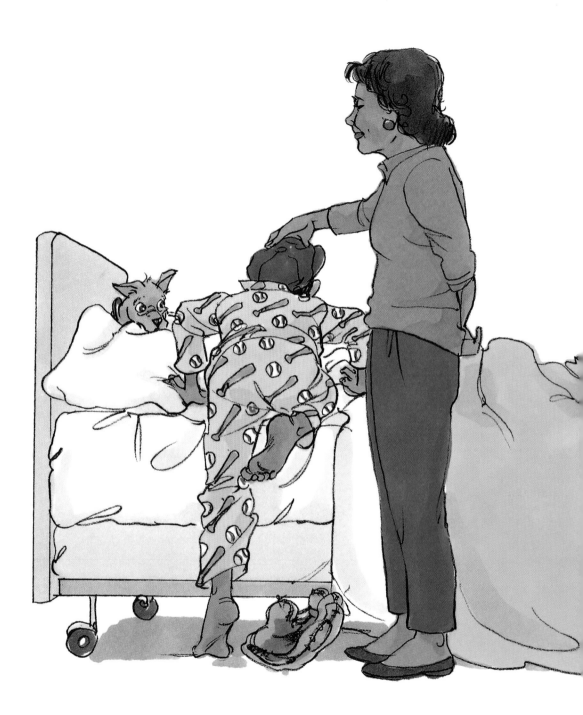

Mom said I looked miserable. She informed me there would no school this morning. And there would definitely be no baseball practice this afternoon.

You just can't fool my mom.

    Mom tucked me back under my covers and stuck a thermometer in my mouth. When she pulled it out again, it read ninety-nine point nine.

    "You have a little **fever,** " she said. "I'll get you some medicine. You try to get some rest."

I didn't want to have a **fever.** So I got some rest. When I woke up, I told Mom I felt great! But she still didn't let me go to baseball practice.

That evening Karen Washington called.
"We missed you today," she reported. "Tim Anderson is working on his **fastball,** but he hasn't quite mastered the grip."

It felt good to know they missed me. It felt good to know they missed my **fastball.**

I just had to get well in time for the game!

I tried to go to sleep early that night. But every time I laid my head down, I started to cough. Mom said if I didn't feel better in the **morning,** she'd take me to see the **doctor.** I finally fell asleep and had a terrific dream about pitching a no-hitter in front of a crowd of thousands!

The next **morning** I felt great! Then I got out of bed. I didn't feel so great anymore.

Mom took me to see the **doctor.**

We arrived at Dr. Elman's office and waited in the waiting room until the nurse came out and called our name. She took us back into an examination room and asked me some questions, then took my **temperature** with a really cool looking thermometer.

She put it in my ear and waited until it went "beep." Then she took it out and smiled.

"Your **temperature** is good," she said.

 She told us Dr. Elman would be in to see us in just a few minutes, then left.

While we waited, I explored the examination room. There were lots of cabinets and a sink with a funny faucet you could turn on by pressing petals with your feet. And there were **posters** on the walls.

One **poster** was about food. Another poster showed where the food goes in your body. But the last poster was the best one I had ever seen!

"That's Cy Young, the greatest pitcher that ever lived."

I whirled around to find **Dr. Elman** standing in the doorway, grinning.

"I just got that poster last week," he continued. "You like it?"

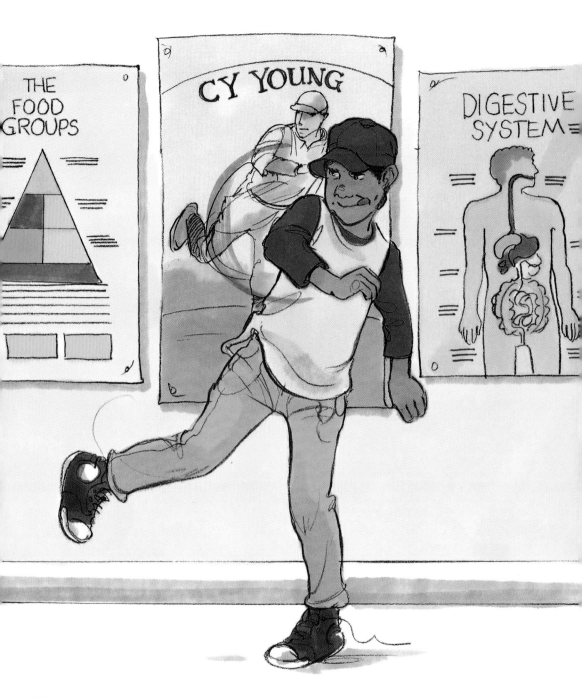

 "Like it?" I said. "I LOVE it! I'm a pitcher too, you know."

Dr. Elman smiled. "Yes, I know."

 I smiled back and eagerly told him that was why he had to make me better today. "I just have to pitch in the first game of the season tomorrow!"

Dr. Elman said couldn't make any promises, but he would do his best. Then he started the examination.

He looked in my ears. He looked in my eyes.
He looked at my throat. He felt my neck. He even
looked up my nose!

Then he used his stethoscope to listen to my heart and told me to take deep breaths while he listened to my lungs.

"What do you hear?" I asked anxiously. "Will I be okay by **tomorrow**?"

"Hmmm . . . I think I hear the roar of the crowd at a baseball game," he answered with a grin.

 "Does that mean I can play **tomorrow**?"

Dr. Elman shook his head. "I'm sorry, Jason," he said. "You will be fine. But not by tomorrow."

He told my mother that it didn't look like anything serious, but he'd like her to keep me in bed over the weekend. Then he turned to me and said, "I wish I knew of some way to get you better in time for the game tomorrow, but I'm afraid there's still no cure for the common cold."

He did wish he could help me. I could tell.

"It's okay, Dr. Elman," I told him. "It's just a game."

Then Mom and I went home.

Saturday morning I woke up feeling pretty lousy. It felt awful knowing that my team was about to start the first game of the season without me. Then I heard the **phone** ring. After a moment, I heard my mom's **voice** calling up to me in my room.

"It's for you, Jason," Mom said.

I picked up the **phone** and said "Hello?"

"Hi, Jason," said a **voice.** "It's Karen!"

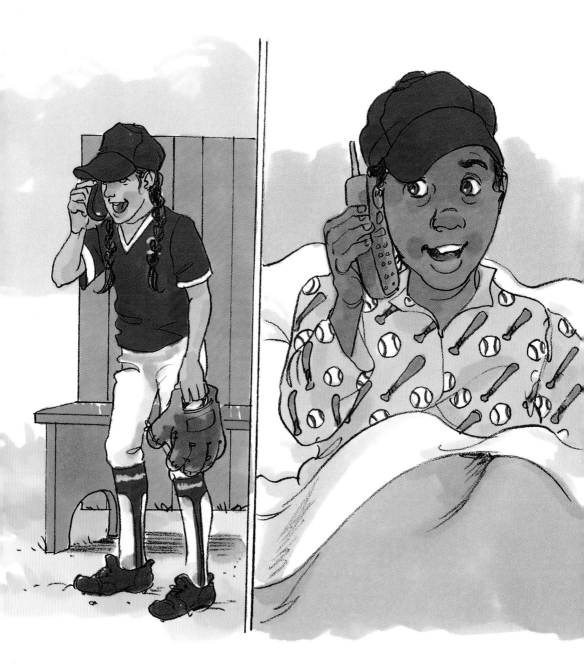

Karen Washington was calling me from the baseball field!
"We're still in the first **inning** of the game," she reported.
"Tim Anderson is pitching and he's doing great! We tagged a
runner out on first and Dan caught a fly ball and Tim actually
struck somebody out!"

"I have to go now," she said. "Coach Bill says
I'm up next! I'll call you back next **inning**."

It was fantastic! Every inning either Karen or Coach Bill or some other team member called up to fill me in on what was happening at the ballpark. It wasn't quite as good as being there in person, but it was pretty close. Even my mom was eager to hear the next report!

Our team played very well. The other team played well, too. But I guess we played better because we won the game!

 Mom said she was really sorry I couldn't be there to celebrate with my friends, but you can't always predict when you're going to get sick.

"It's okay," I said. "There will be lots of other games."

Playing ball is really fun. So is winning. But the very best part of baseball is having such good, good friends.

If you liked
***Baseball Fever*, here are two other**
***We Both Read*® Books you are sure to enjoy!**

Explore the vast regions of space in the newest nonfiction book in our series. The book provides facinating information, as well as spectacular photographs of planets, moons, stars, and galaxies. The new space station and how astronauts live in space are other topics covered in this book that is sure to be popular with adults and children alike.